The Funny Baby

DEAR CAREGIVER,

The *Beginning-to-Read* series is a carefully written collection of classic readers you may remember from your own childhood. Each book features text comprised of common sight words to provide your child ample practice reading the words that appear most frequently in written text. The many additional details in the pictures enhance the story and offer the opportunity for you to help your child expand oral language and develop comprehension.

Begin by reading the story to your child, followed by letting him or her read familiar words and soon your child will be able to read the story independently. At each step of the way, be sure to praise your reader's efforts to build his or her confidence as an independent reader. Discuss the pictures and encourage your child to make connections between the story and his or her own life. At the end of the story, you will find reading activities and a word list that will help your child practice and strengthen beginning reading skills.

Above all, the most important part of the reading experience is to have fun and enjoy it!

Shannon Cannon

Shannon Cannon,
Literacy Consultant

Norwood House Press • P.O. Box 316598 • Chicago, Illinois 60631
For more information about Norwood House Press please visit our website at *www.norwoodhousepress.com* or call 866-565-2900.

LIBRARY OF CONGRESS CATALOGING-IN-PUBLICATION DATA

Hillert, Margaret.
  The funny baby : The ugly duckling retold / by Margaret Hillert;
illustrated by Hertha Depper. — Rev. and expanded library ed.
     p. cm. — (Beginning-to-read book)
  Summary: An ugly duckling spends an unhappy year ostracized by the other
animals before he grows into a beautiful swan. Includes reading activities.
  ISBN-13: 978-1-59953-048-2 (library binding : alk. paper)
  ISBN-10: 1-59953-048-1 (library binding : alk. paper)
  [1. Fairy tales.] I. Depper, Hertha, ill. II. Andersen, H. C. (Hans
Christian), 1805-1875. Grimme flling. English. III. Title. IV. Series:
Hillert, Margaret. Beginning to read series. Fairy tales and folklore.
  PZ8.H5425Fu 2007
  [E]—dc22   2006007895

A Beginning-to-Read Book

The Funny Baby

by Margaret Hillert

Illustrated by Hertha Depper

NORWOODHOUSE PRESS

Oh, look.
Here is something.
One little one.
Two little ones.
Three little ones.
And a big one.

Where is the mother?
Can you find the mother?

See here.
Here is the mother.
See mother go.

Look, look.
Mother is here.

Oh, my. Oh, my.
Look in here.
One little one.
Two little ones.
Three little ones.

And—
One big one!

One yellow one.
Two yellow ones.
Three yellow ones.

And—
One is not yellow!
It is not my baby.

Away we go.
We can play.
It is fun to play.

Here I come.
Here I come.
I want to play.

Not you, not you.
You look funny.
Go away.
You can not play.

Oh my, oh my.
I look funny.
I can not play.

I look funny.
I can not help it.
Where can I go?

Away I go.
Away, away, away.

Look up here.
Something is yellow.
Something is red.

Oh, oh, oh.
Look down here.
It is not fun.
Help me. Help me.

Look, look!
See me.
Oh, my!
Away I go!

Look in here.
See me.
It is fun.

Look, look!
Oh, my.
I see something.
Something big.

Oh, oh, oh.
Look down here.
See me.
See me.
See big, big me.

Away we go!
Away, away, away.

The following activities support the findings of the National Reading Panel that determined the most effective components for reading instruction are: Phonemic Awareness, Phonics, Vocabulary, Fluency, and Text Comprehension.

Phonemic Awareness: The /u/ sound

Sound Substitution: Say the words on the left to your child. Ask your child to repeat the word, changing the middle sound to /**u**/:

fin = fun	cap = cup	mad = mud	bat = but
lick = luck	dig = dug	shot = shut	rib = rub
fizz = fuzz	track = truck	bin = bun	rag = rug
snag = snug	lamp = lump	stamp = stump	

Phonics: The letter Uu

1. Demonstrate how to form the letters **U** and **u** for your child.
2. Have your child practice writing **U** and **u** at least three times each.
3. Ask your child to point to the words in the book that have the letter **u** in them.
4. Write down the following words and ask your child to circle the letter **u** in each word:

you	fluff	funny	run	loud	duck
bus	sound	fur	nut	shut	caught
up	such	under	round	plump	pup

Vocabulary: Adjectives

1. Explain to your child that words that describe something are called adjectives.
2. Say the following adjectives and ask your child to name something that the adjective might describe:

funny	little	tall	short	cuddly	pretty
big	silly	cute	noisy	furry	soft

3. Write the words on sticky note paper.

4. Read each word aloud for your child.

5. Mix the words up randomly and say each word to your child. Ask your child to point to the correct word.

Fluency: Shared Reading

1. Reread the story to your child at least two more times while your child tracks the print by running a finger under the words as they are read. Ask your child to read the words he or she knows with you.

2. Reread the story taking turns, alternating readers between sentences or pages.

Text Comprehension: Discussion Time

1. Ask your child to retell the sequence of events in the story.

2. To check comprehension, ask your child the following questions:

- Why did the mother think the big baby wasn't hers?
- Why did the funny baby leave?
- How do you think the funny baby felt when he could not play?
- What happened to the funny baby?
- What is the lesson in the story?

WORD LIST

The Funny Baby uses the 40 words listed below.

This list can be used to practice reading the words that appear in the text. You may wish to write the words on index cards and use them to help your child build automatic word recognition. Regular practice with these words will enhance your child's fluency in reading connected text.

a	help	oh	want
and	here	one	we
away			where
	I	play	
baby	in		yellow
big	is	red	you
	it		
can		see	
come	little	something	
	look		
down		the	
	me	three	
find	mother	to	
fun	my	two	
funny			
	not	up	
go			

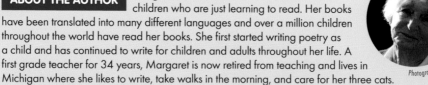

ABOUT THE AUTHOR Margaret Hillert has written over 80 books for children who are just learning to read. Her books have been translated into many different languages and over a million children throughout the world have read her books. She first started writing poetry as a child and has continued to write for children and adults throughout her life. A first grade teacher for 34 years, Margaret is now retired from teaching and lives in Michigan where she likes to write, take walks in the morning, and care for her three cats.

Photograph by Glenna Washburn

ABOUT THE ADVISER Shannon Cannon contributed the activities pages that appear in this book. Shannon serves as a literacy consultant and provides staff development to help improve reading instruction. She is a frequent presenter at educational conferences and workshops. Prior to this she worked as an elementary school teacher and as president of a curriculum publishing company.